THE
NIGHT
BEFORE
CHRISTMAS
IN
CHICAGO

Text
Bryce Taylor

Illustrations
Steve Egan

Dust Jacket Illustration
Shauna Mooney Kawasaki

Y

ISBN 0-87905-488-3
prpk 10: 0-87905-527-8

Published by
Gibbs Smith, Publisher
P.O. Box 667
Layton, Utah 84041

03 02 01 00   11 10 9 8
Copyright © 1992
by Gibbs Smith, Publisher

'Twas the night

before Christmas,

and all

'round the loop

The evening news

broadcast

the late

weather scoop.

The word was

not cheery;

there seemed

to be proof

'Twould be

no St. Nick

on the

Second City roof.

For a big wind

was whipping off

Lake Michigan,

And threatened to

stop him before

he'd begun.

A team through

this skyline

could scarce

navigate,

So the

weatherfolks

felt he would

just have to wait.

The shoppers

at Field's

heard the news

in despair.

"What's Christmas,

if Santa Claus

cannot be there?"

And children . . .

the children

were all

in a stew;

They couldn't

imagine what

Santa would do.

It was certainly

clear they would

not go to bed,

With that team

in the sky

and St. Nick

at its head.

Some folks down

on Rush Street

were seeking

good cheer,

But the fun

couldn't start

with this great

crisis near.

So the evening

wore on,

and the people

grew teary.

This was worse

than the cow

and poor

Mrs. O'Leary.

But there,

in the sky,

flying fast

through the air . . .

A speck.

Just a plane

flying into

O'Hare?

No!

Santa was

coming to futures

mark holders;

To the streets

of Chicago;

to the Town

of Broad Shoulders.

'Round the Hancock,

past Amoco,

with a whoop

and a holler,

But the giant

Sears Tower

simply seemed

to loom taller . . .

When a gust

swept him past

with just inches

to spare.

He had just

enough time

to leave good

wishes there,

Then the sleigh

bumped the side

of the

Merchandise Mart

And was grounded

right there;

it could not

get a start

'Cause the wind

held it down.

Santa leaped from

the sleigh.

"Just call

Mayor Daley,

the one with the J.

"If I know

Chicago,

he'll easily

resolve it.

"It's just politics.

Why, I'm sure

he can solve it!"

"But Santa,"

the people cried,

eyes getting large,

"It's now

Mr. Richard M. Daley

in charge."

Poor Santa's

face fell;

it was getting

so late.

"How about the

expressway?

Perhaps the

Tri-state,

"The Stevenson,

Kennedy,

maybe the Ryan,

The Edens

or Eisenhower . . .

soon I'd be flying!"

But a traffic

reporter said,

"Sorry, St. Nick.

"The expressways

are packed and

the traffic is thick."

It seemed nothing

would work.

It seemed

no one could do it,

When a voice

loudly stated,

"Why there's just

nothing to it."

"Who are you?"

asked Santa,

"A giant, I think."

"Just call me

'Air Jordan',"

he said with

a wink.

They sped off

down Michigan,

passed Water

Tower there,

Then they soared

and they rose —

Santa, reindeer,

and 'Air.'

They flew!

And was that

Wrigley Field

off their bow?

It might be . . .

It could be . . .

It was!

Holy Cow!

"Chicago,"

called Santa,

"Merry Christmas

and the like!"

Said Dasher

to Dancer,

"Why can't we

be like Mike?"